CHICO BON BON™
MONKEY WITH A TOOL BELT

GEAR UP AND GO!

Adapted by Ximena Hastings
Episode written by Bob Boyle & Frank Rocco
Based on the TV show *Chico Bon Bon: Monkey with a Tool Belt*

SIMON SPOTLIGHT
New York London Toronto Sydney New Delhi

SIMON SPOTLIGHT
An imprint of Simon & Schuster Children's Publishing Division
1230 Avenue of the Americas, New York, New York 10020
This Simon Spotlight edition September 2021

For information about special discounts for bulk purchases, please contact Simon & Schuster Special Sales
at 1-866-506-1949 or business@simonandschuster.com.
Manufactured in the United States of America 0821 LAK
2 4 6 8 10 9 7 5 3 1
ISBN 978-1-5344-8968-4
ISBN 978-1-5344-8969-1 (ebook)

It was an ordinary day in the city of Blunderburg. Clark was busy organizing his peanut collection by using a **SUPER PEANUT STACKER**. He rolled a big peanut down the Stacker's slide, where it rolled into a hole with other big peanuts.

"Now all the big peanuts are together, all the medium peanuts are together, and all the small peanuts are together," Clark said. "It's like magic!"

“That’s not magic! That’s called **SORTING**,” Rainbow Thunder said. “Sorting is a way to organize things by shape, color, or size. You’re sorting your peanuts by size!”

“Wow, sorting is way cooler than magic!” Clark said.

Ring, ring! Just then the banana phone rang. Tiny, Clark, and Rainbow Thunder gathered in the mission control room.

Chico Bon Bon walked in a few seconds later. "I've got a problem! Can you help me solve it?" he cried. "I'm missing . . . **A SOCK!**"

"Uh, is that all?" Rainbow Thunder asked.

"This is an emergency!" Chico said. "I've **NEVER** taken my socks off. Not since I was a little baby monkey!"

"This is a **SOCK-MERGENCY**!" Clark said. "But don't worry, I think I know where your lost sock is."

“Whenever someone loses a sock, it goes where all lost socks go: **SOCK MOUNTAIN**!” Clark said.

He pulled out a book and showed everyone a picture of a tall, wobbly mountain. Then he turned the page to reveal a map.

The Fix-It Force gathered their tools and left Bon Bon Labs. It was time for their **SOCK QUEST** to begin!

The Fix-It Force followed the map through Blunderburg, where they ran into several residents who needed help. One of Mrs. Coleslaw's newly knitted **SMALL PURPLE SOCKS** had disappeared. Mayor Murphy had lost her royal sock, too! All the people of Blunderburg were worried about their lost socks.

"Don't worry, everyone. We know exactly where all the socks are!" Chico said confidently.

The Fix-It Force continued on their way. They traveled through the desert of **CRABBY CANYON**, over the tall **VULTURE VOLCANO**, and across the tasty **DESSERT ISLAND**.

Finally, they reached **SOCK MOUNTAIN**!

Chico and Rainbow Thunder dove into the mountain to find everyone's missing socks. But suddenly, the Fix-It Force heard loud stomping. A giant orange creature appeared in front of them!

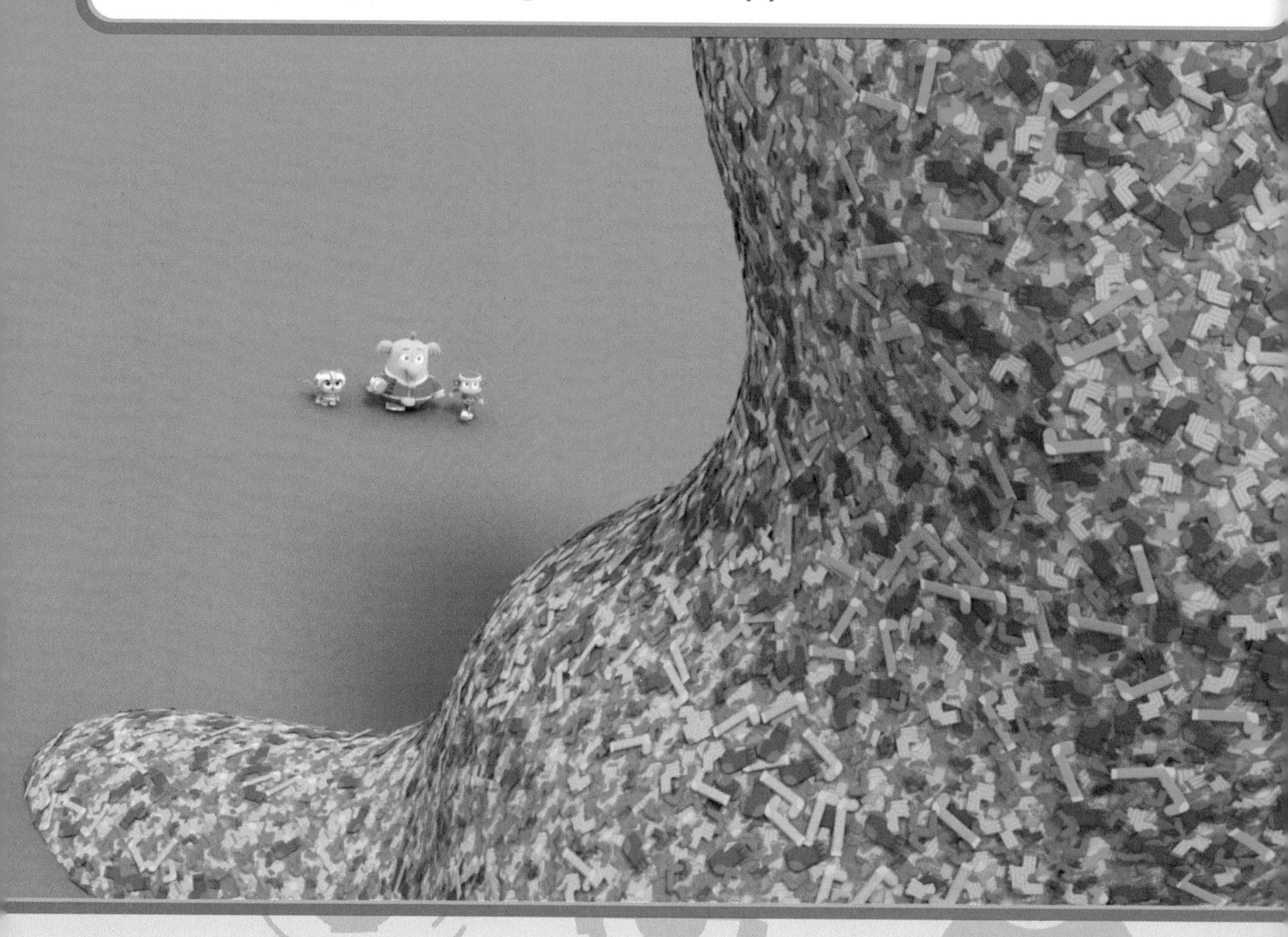

Clark's book explained that the creature was a **GIANT SOCKTOPUS** who takes everyone's socks. "The book also says that sweet singing soothes the savage socktopus to sleep," Clark said, and began to sing a lullaby.

Soon, the scary socktopus was peacefully asleep.

"Now, let's get this sock situation straightened out!" Chico said.

Chico and the team started by looking for Mrs. Coleslaw's small purple sock. Clark found a big purple sock, and Tiny found a small purple sock with toes, but neither one was the right one.

"This is going to take **FOREVER**!" Chico cried.

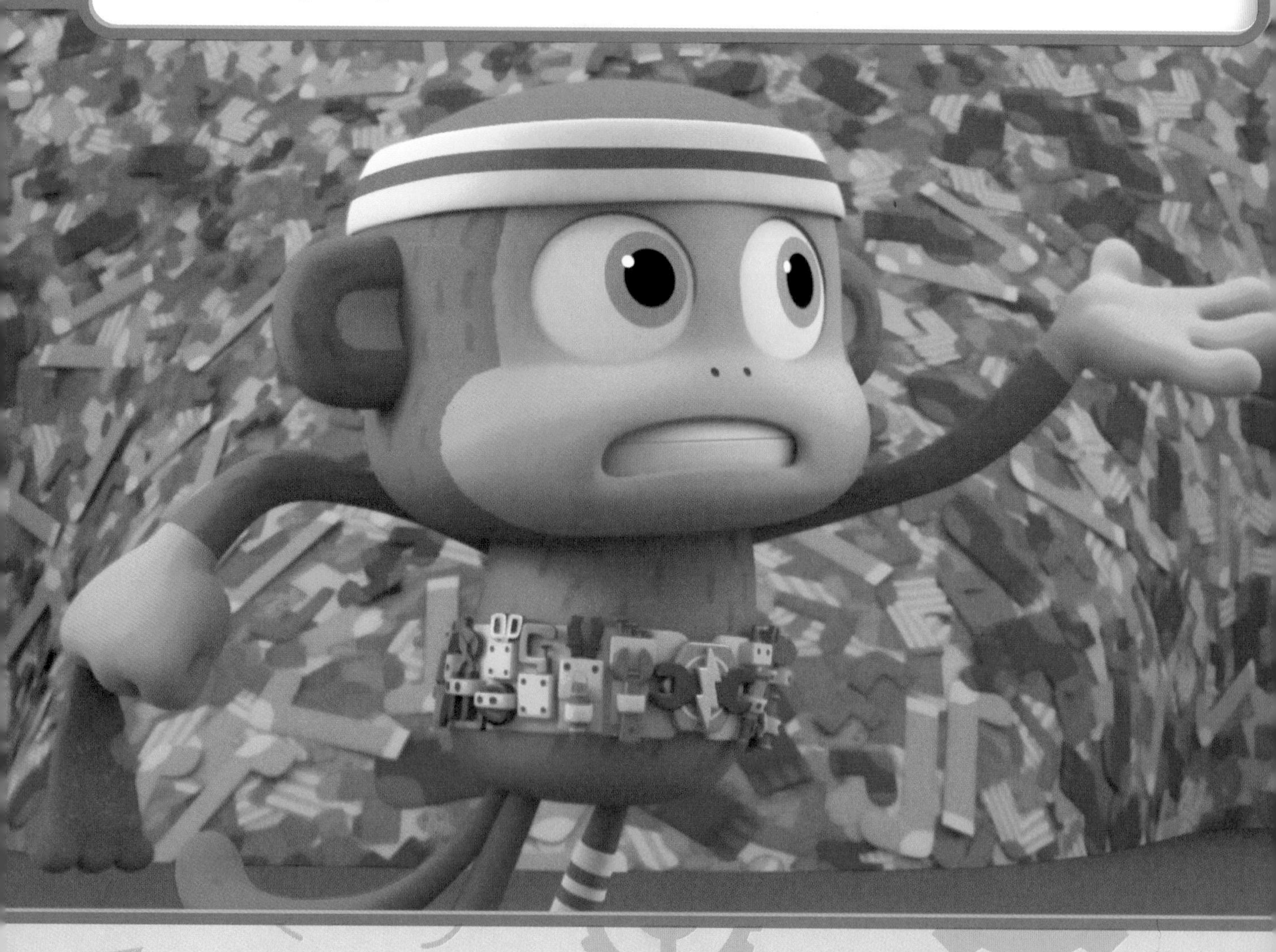

Chico decided to take a banana break. He needed to find a way to organize all the mixed-up socks.

"This is just like when I was sorting my peanuts," Clark commented.

"Blazing bananas! That's it!" Chico said. "We can build a **SUPER SOCK SORTER MACHINE!**"

The Fix-It Force began building the Super Sock Sorter. Soon, they were ready to give it a try. Tiny pulled the lever, and the machine began to sort the socks into piles by **SIZE**, by **SHAPE**, and by **COLOR**.

With the Super Sock Sorter's help, the Fix-It Force found everyone's lost socks . . . except Chico's.

Then Chico noticed his sock was dangling on the sleeping socktopus's tentacle. Chico grabbed it back, but he accidentally woke up the sleeping socktopus! Once it noticed the missing sock, it began to **ROAR**.

"Oh no! We don't have any socks left to replace Chico's!" Rainbow Thunder said.

Luckily, Mrs. Coleslaw helped by knitting plenty of socks for the socktopus. It giggled happily.

"I can't believe we found Sock Mountain and met a socktopus!" Chico said.

THE FIX-IT FORCE HAD SAVED THE DAY ONCE AGAIN!